ISBN 978-1-60309-068-1
1. Children's Books
2. Donuts
3. Graphic Novels

Published by Top Shelf Productions, PO BOX 1282, Marietta, GA. 30061-1282, USA. Publishers: Brett Warnock and Chris Staros.

Visit our online catalog at www.topshelfcomix.com. First printing June 2011. Printed in Singapore.

There's a little place in town that you should know...
OKIE DOKIE DONUTS
OPEN
SALE
HOT!
...It's a hot donut service that's sure to grow.

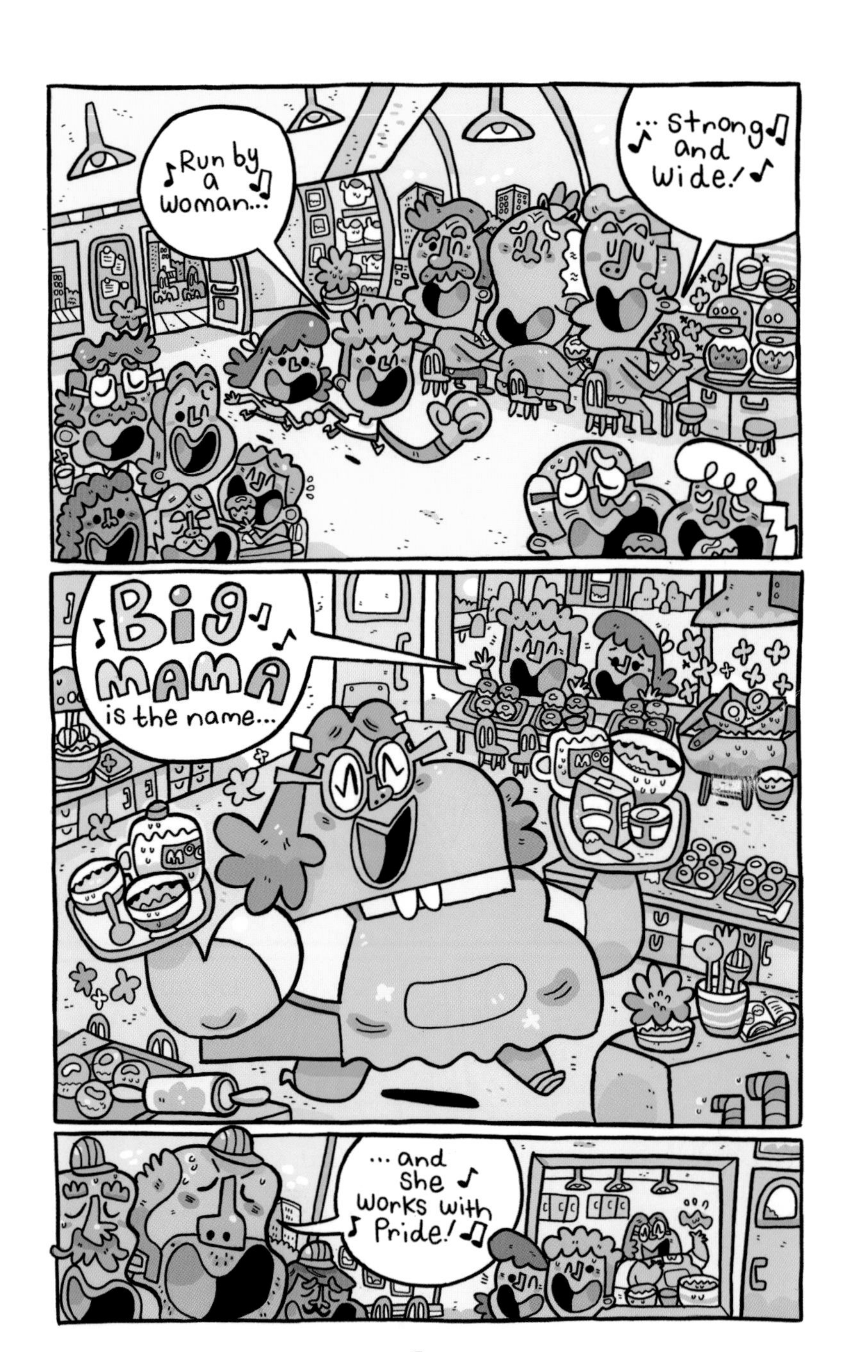
Run by a woman...
... Strong and wide!
Big MAMA is the name...
... and she works with Pride!

Every little donut is made just right...
So it doesn't really matter which one you bite!
yellow batter goes right in the bowl...
...Hot out of the oven, and we're on a roll!

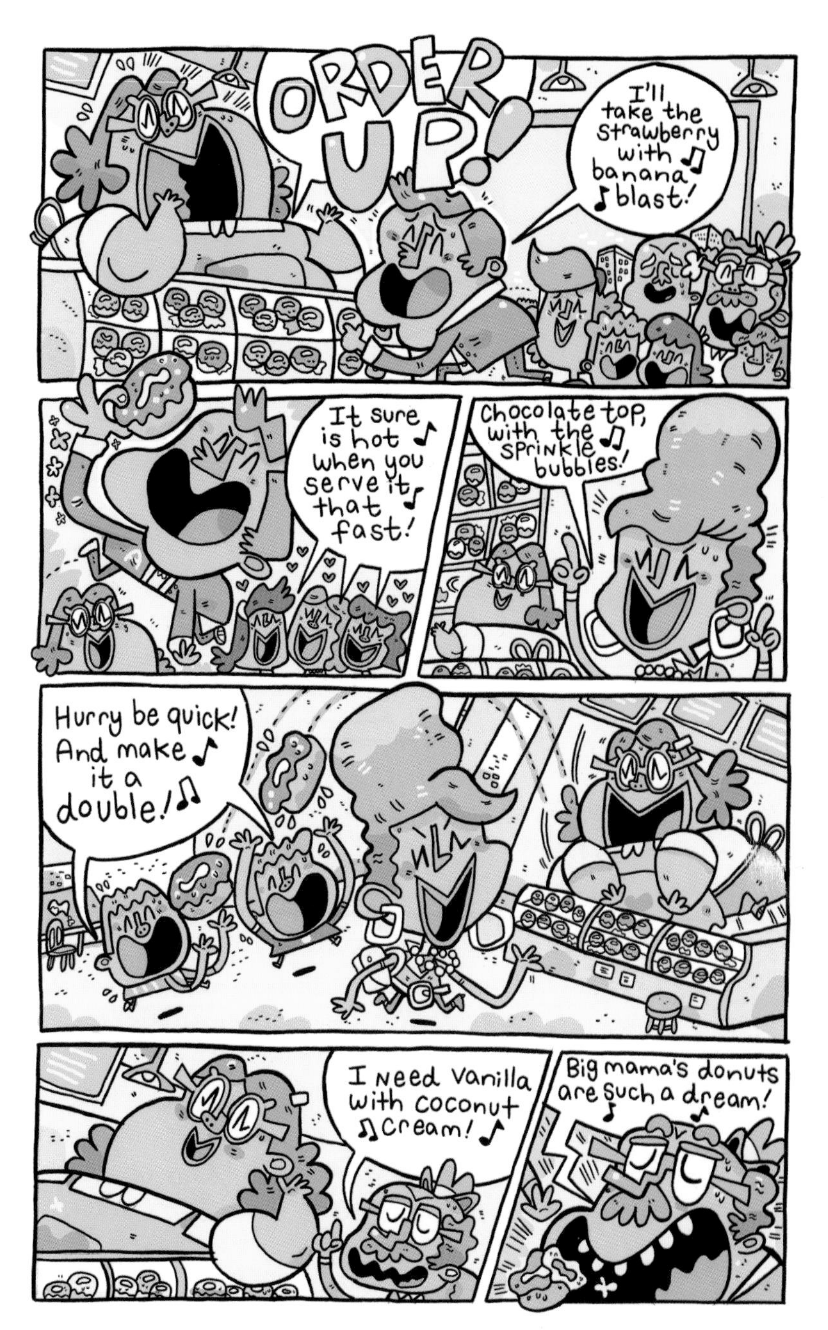
ORDER UP!
I'll take the strawberry with ♫ banana ♪ blast!
It sure is hot ♪ when you serve it ♪ that fast!
Chocolate top, with the ♫ sprinkle bubbles!
Hurry be quick! And make ♪ it a double! ♫
I need vanilla with coconut ♫ cream! ♪
Big mama's donuts are such a dream! ♪ ♪

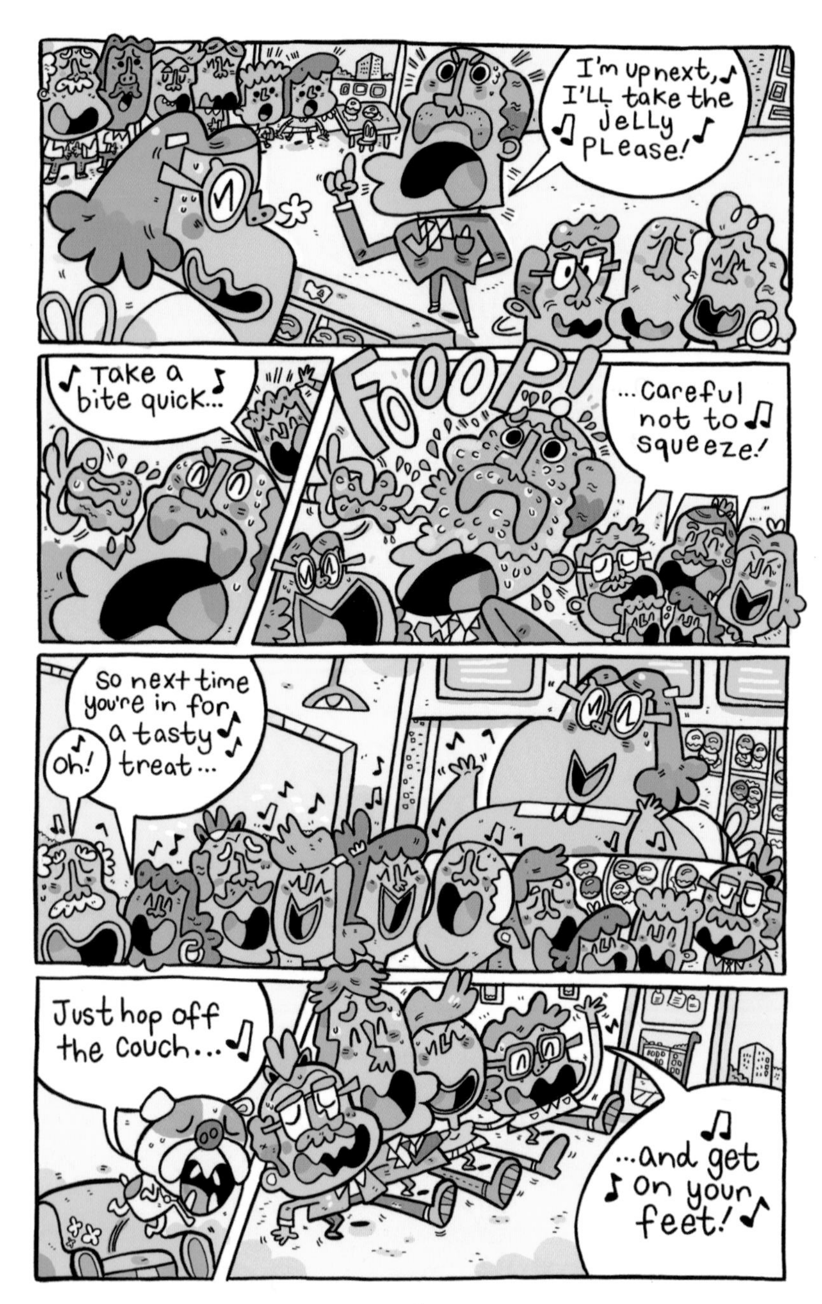
I'm up next, I'LL take the JeLLy PLease!
Take a bite quick...
FOOOP!
...Careful not to squeeze!
So next time you're in for a tasty treat...
Oh!
Just hop off the couch...
...and get on your feet!

Don't push...
Don't PULL...
Don't run or shove!
Big mama's got donuts...
...and they're made with LOVE!

Story 1

GC CO.

CO.

Whew, what a manic morning!
The breakfast crowd is always a sweat!
Thanks for helping out, Henry!
NO problemo, Big mama!
TOSS
Shoooo
POK
Shoooo
POK
Oh yeah!
TA-DA!

RRRR
Henry! watch out for that Vacuum cord!
RRRR
RRRR
SNAG
OOOF
GASP
Hopping Hoovers!
Henry, you're the best assistant I've ever had...
...but sometimes I wonder...
...if you make more mess than you clean up!

maybe I should hire more help around here.
An extra pair of hands sure would go a long way!
But who would want to work here?
OPEN
Hark! Did I just hear a restaurateur in trouble?!

Pink Sprinkles! who are you?!
The name's mr. may-weather!
I sell Products that make your grueling kitchen chores go by in a breeze!
For over 14 years I've been Providing Portable plug-ins no patisserie can do without!
I represent the "Great Cooks Cooking corporation!"
"The same great taste, at twice the haste!"
you might have heard of some of our Products... The Spaghetti wiggler!
?!
The mush master 9000!
and Dr. Goodlesuit's fantasic Noodle Shooter!

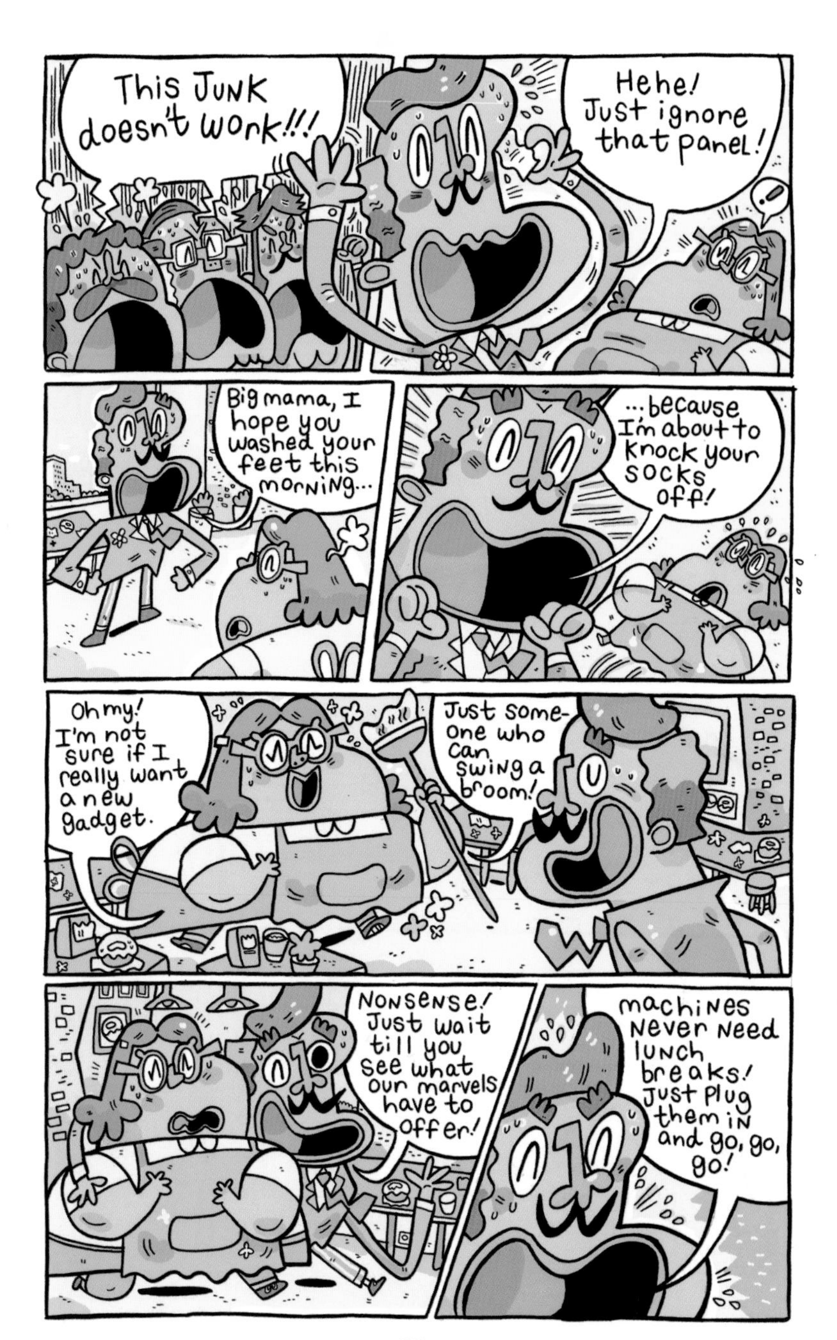
This JUNK doesn't WORK!!!
Hehe! Just ignore that panel!
Big mama, I hope you washed your feet this morning...
...because I'm about to knock your socks off!
Oh my! I'm not sure if I really want a new gadget.
Just someone who can swing a broom!
NONSENSE! Just wait till you see what our marvels have to offer!
machines never need lunch breaks! Just plug them in and go, go, go!

I don't need short-cuts. I make everything with Love!
a machine wouldn't know how to do that!
If you can set aside your Pastry punditry for just one moment.
...you'll see how efficient our machines are!
Let's go back to your kitchen. I have a surprise for you!
WASH YOUR PAWS
SPOONS for you
MOO COW! FARM

Ta-da! I've already made the delivery!
GREAT COOKS COOKING CORP
How did you get that giant box in my kitchen?!
It's a comic book! Don't worry about it!
GREAT COOKS COOK
Alright! Let's open this puppy up!
SMASH
What on Earth is that?

Big mama, I want you to meet, MR. Baker! Brilliant Apparatus kooks every Recipe!
FOOSH
The latest in high-tech oven machinery!
Invented by the Great cooks cooking labs!
They spend hours developing new technology!
We've culled the top scientific minds to come up with time-saving culinary concoctions!
Did you add the safety gloves yet?
That's not my job! Someone else do it!

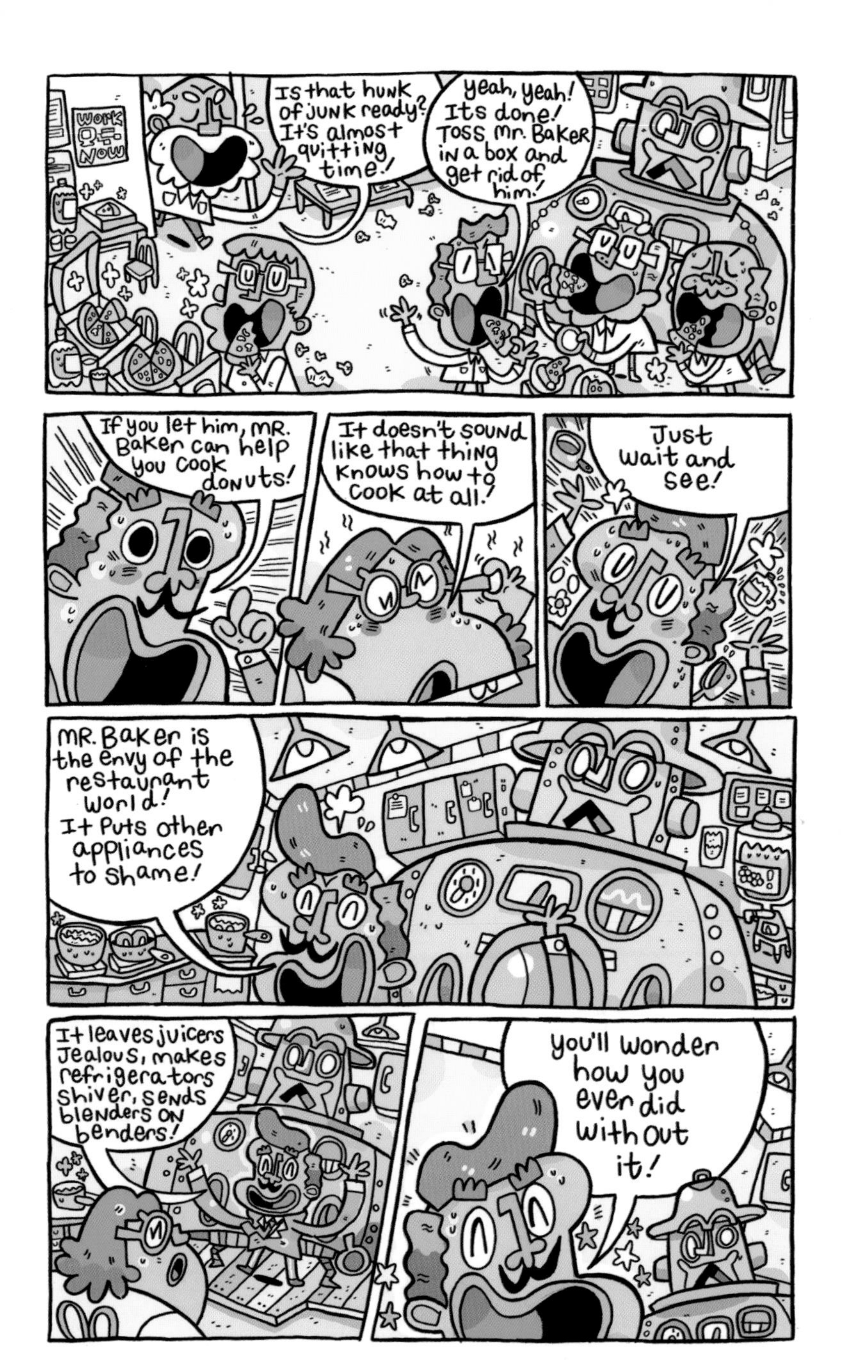
WORK NOW
Is that hunk of junk ready? It's almost quitting time!
Yeah, yeah! Its done! Toss Mr. Baker in a box and get rid of him!
If you let him, Mr. Baker can help you cook donuts!
It doesn't sound like that thing knows how to cook at all.
Just wait and see!
Mr. Baker is the envy of the restaurant world! It puts other appliances to shame!
It leaves juicers jealous, makes refrigerators shiver, sends blenders on benders!
You'll wonder how you ever did without it!

But how does it work?
MR. Baker will cook over 1000 donuts in 40 seconds!
It will powder your dough!
whisk any batter!
glaze any cake!
That doesn't answer my question!
Listen up, Big mama.
I like you, so I'll cut you a deal!
I'll let you try out MR. Baker this afternoon.
Give him a test run!
I think you'll find your restaurant pumping out oodles of strudels in no time!

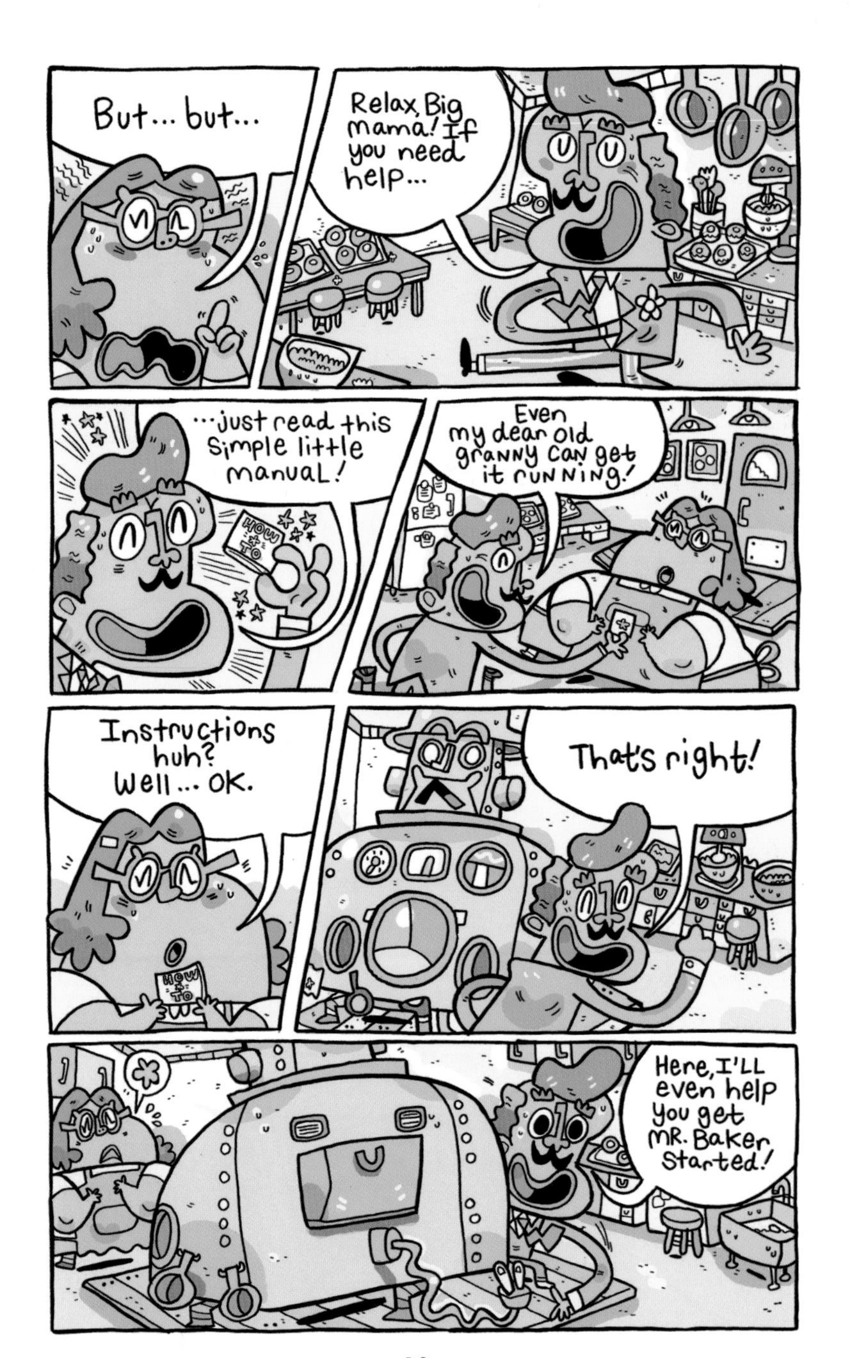
But... but...
Relax, Big mama! If you need help...
...just read this simple little manual!
Even my dear old granny can get it running!
HOW TO
Instructions huh? Well... OK.
That's right!
Here, I'll even help you get Mr. Baker started!

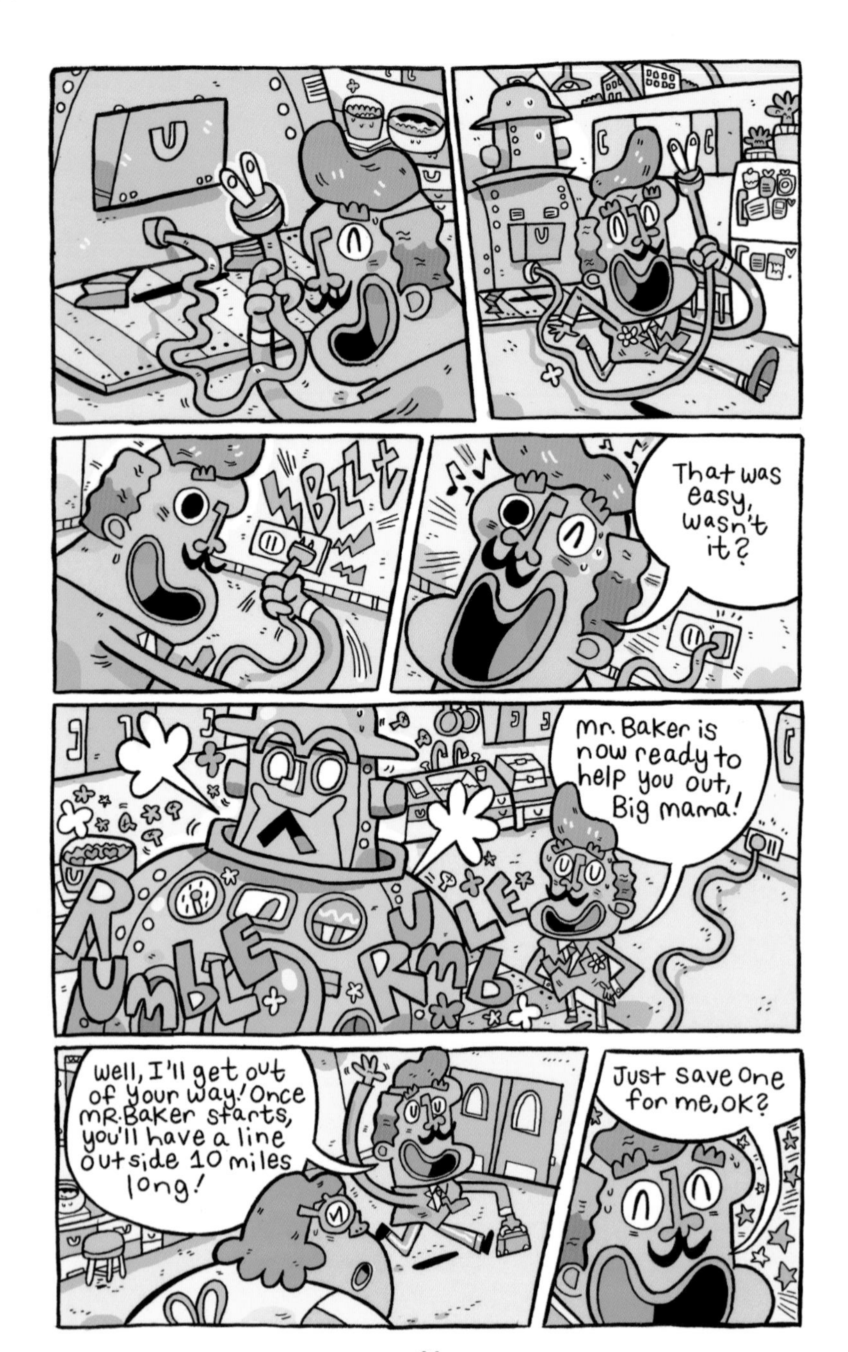
SBZZT
That was easy, wasn't it?
Mr. Baker is now ready to help you out, Big mama!
RUMBLE RUMBLE
Well, I'll get out of your way! Once MR. Baker starts, you'll have a line outside 10 miles long!
Just save one for me, OK?

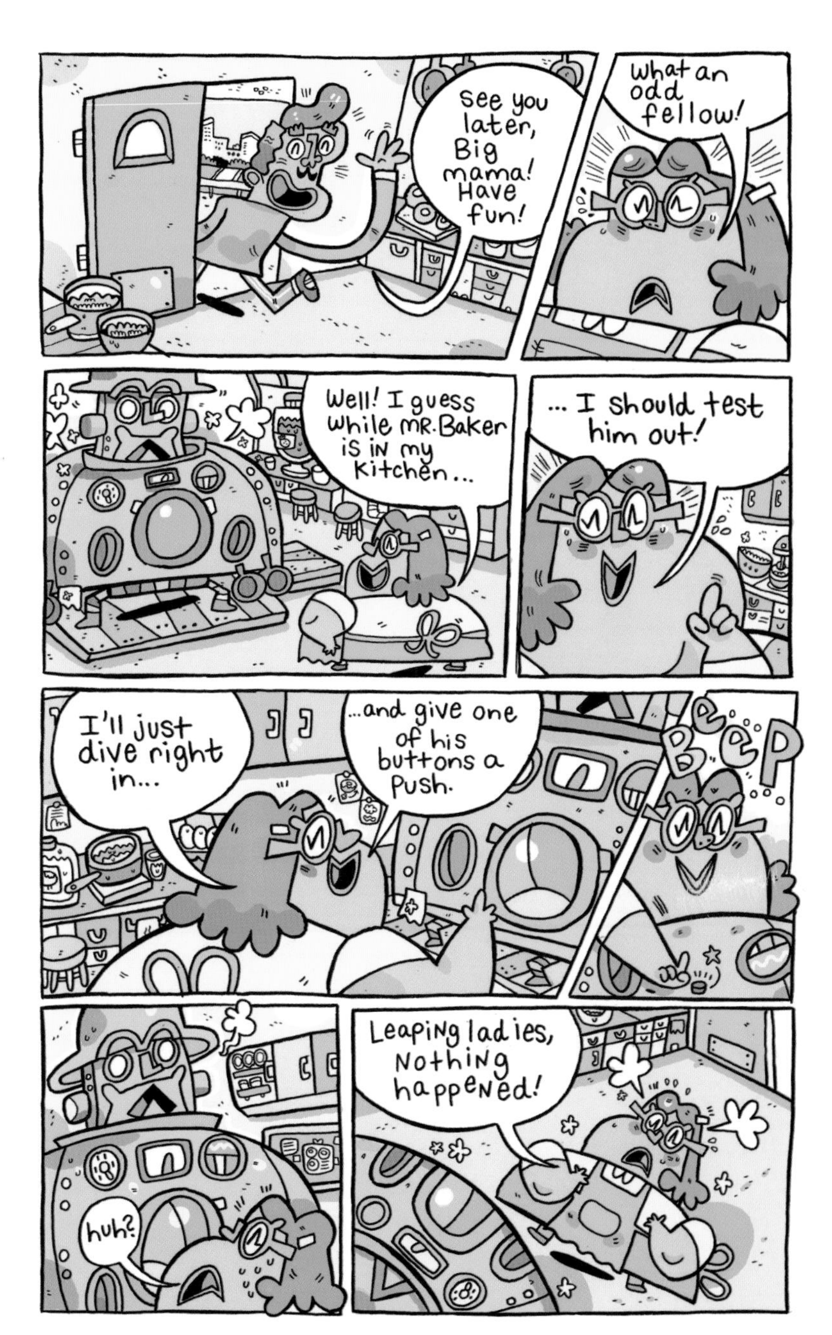
See you later, Big mama! Have fun!
What an odd fellow!
Well! I guess while MR. Baker is in my Kitchen...
... I should test him out!
I'll just dive right in...
...and give one of his buttons a push.
BeeP
huh?
Leaping ladies, Nothing happened!

maybe I didn't push hard enough!
BEEP
BEEP
BLOOP
come on, you lazy metal man! Why won't you WORK?!!
Oh! I KNOW! I'll read the INSTRUCTIONS!
HOW TO
Oh! The manual folds out!
This is so complicated!

Albert Einstein couldn't read this!
I can't make heads or tails from this home-work!
Insert slot left B to slot right G. Press and hold, "up, up."
Big mama, where should I toss this smelly garbage?
Oh, just put it anywhere!
I don't have time to deal with that rotten pile!
Whatever you say, boss!
!

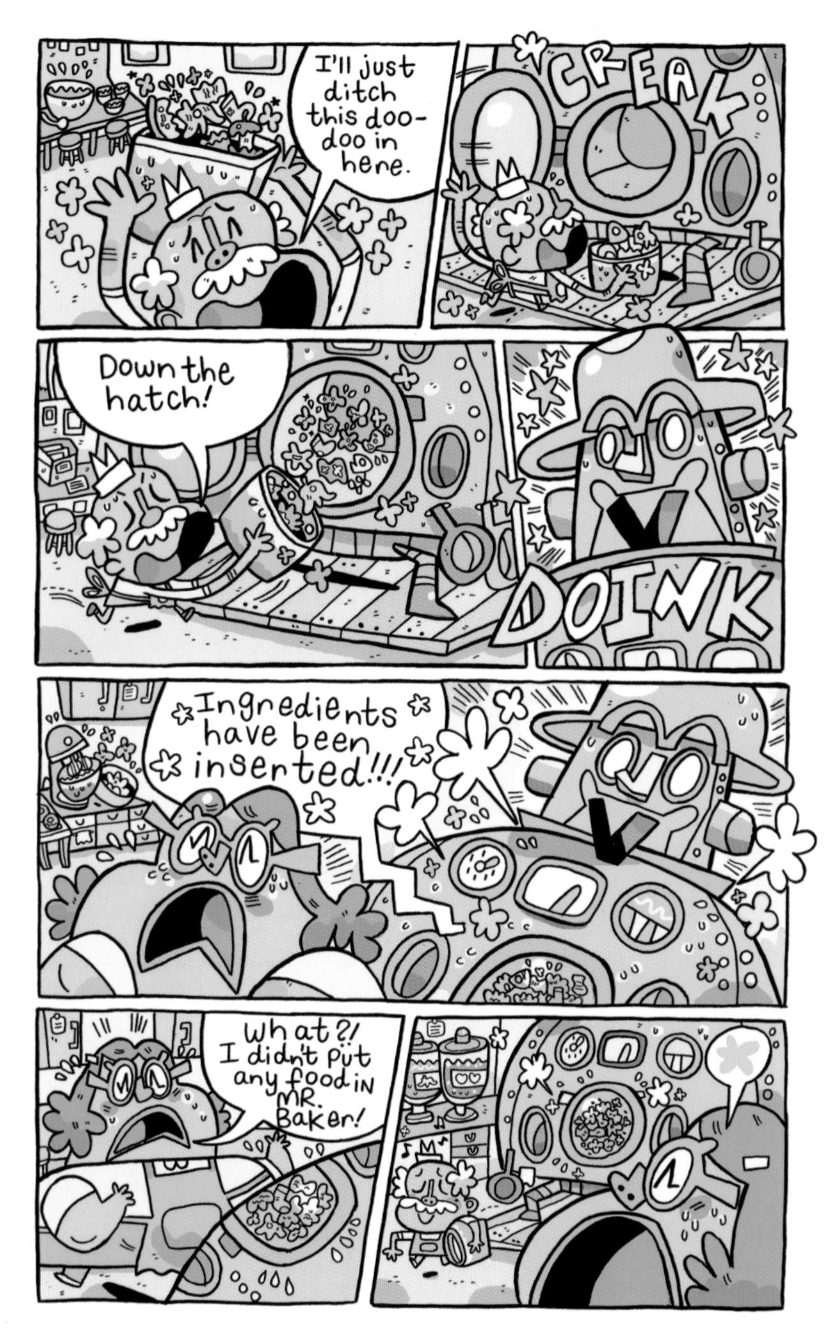
I'll just ditch this doo-doo in here.
CREAK
Down the hatch!
DOINK
Ingredients have been inserted!!!
What?! I didn't put any food in MR. Baker!

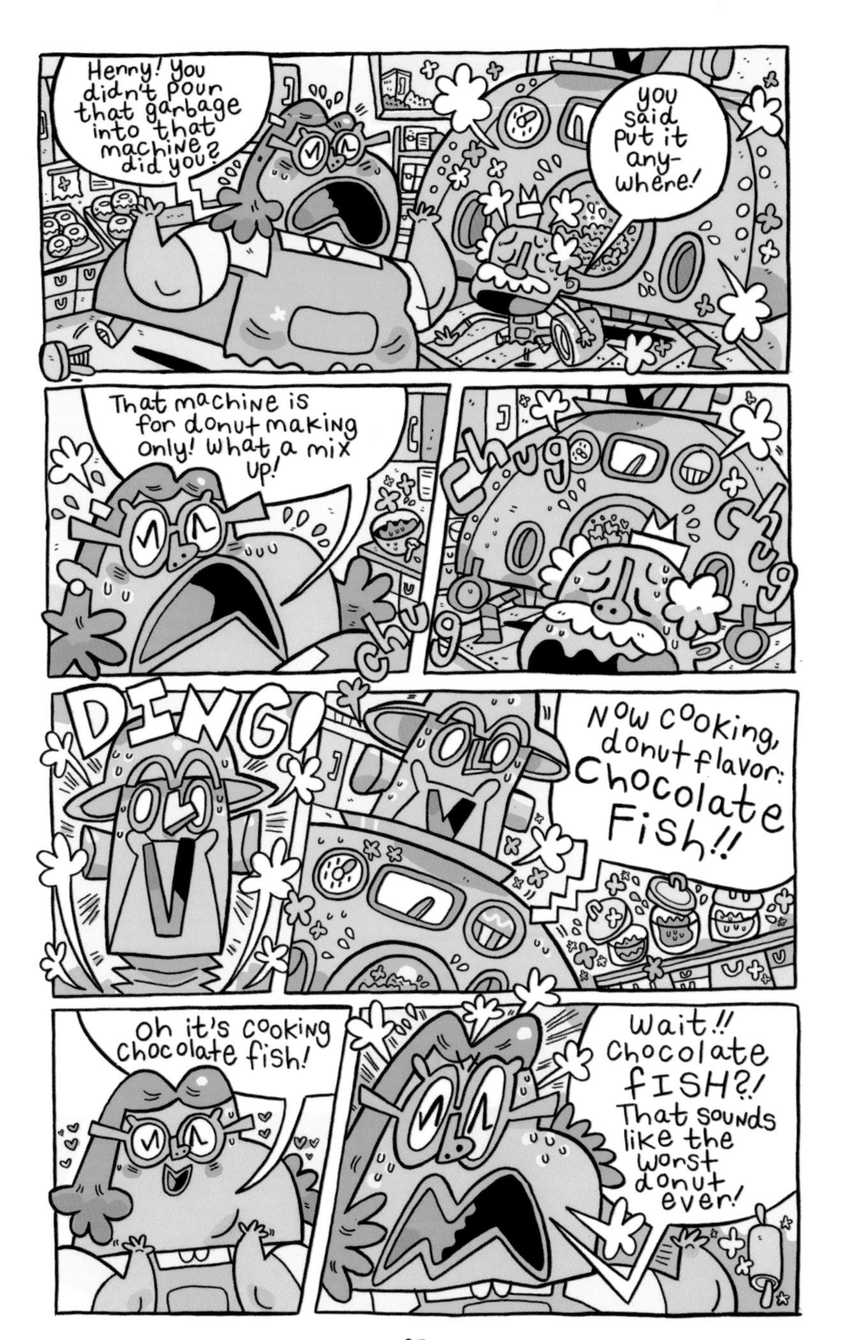
Henny! You didn't pour that garbage into that machine, did you?
You said put it any-where!
That machine is for donut making only! What a mix up!
chug chug chug chug
DING!
Now cooking, donut flavor: Chocolate Fish!!
Oh it's cooking chocolate fish!
Wait!! Chocolate FISH?! That sounds like the worst donut ever!

RUMBLE
UZZZZZZ
ZZZZZ
POP!
POP!
What are the arms for?
UZZZt
cooking sequence under way...
maybe it wants to give us high fives?
POP
SPLOSH
...Taking out the donuts!

TA~DA~~!
Did he just Pull that donut out of his head?

PLOP
Order is now ready! Enjoy!
TOSS!
YUCK! That fish hit me in the face!
Ew! MR. Baker's donuts smell like garbage, too!
Didn't your mom ever tell you not to throw food?
SPLAT!
HA HA HA HA!
GRRRR
This rude robot doesn't know when to quit!

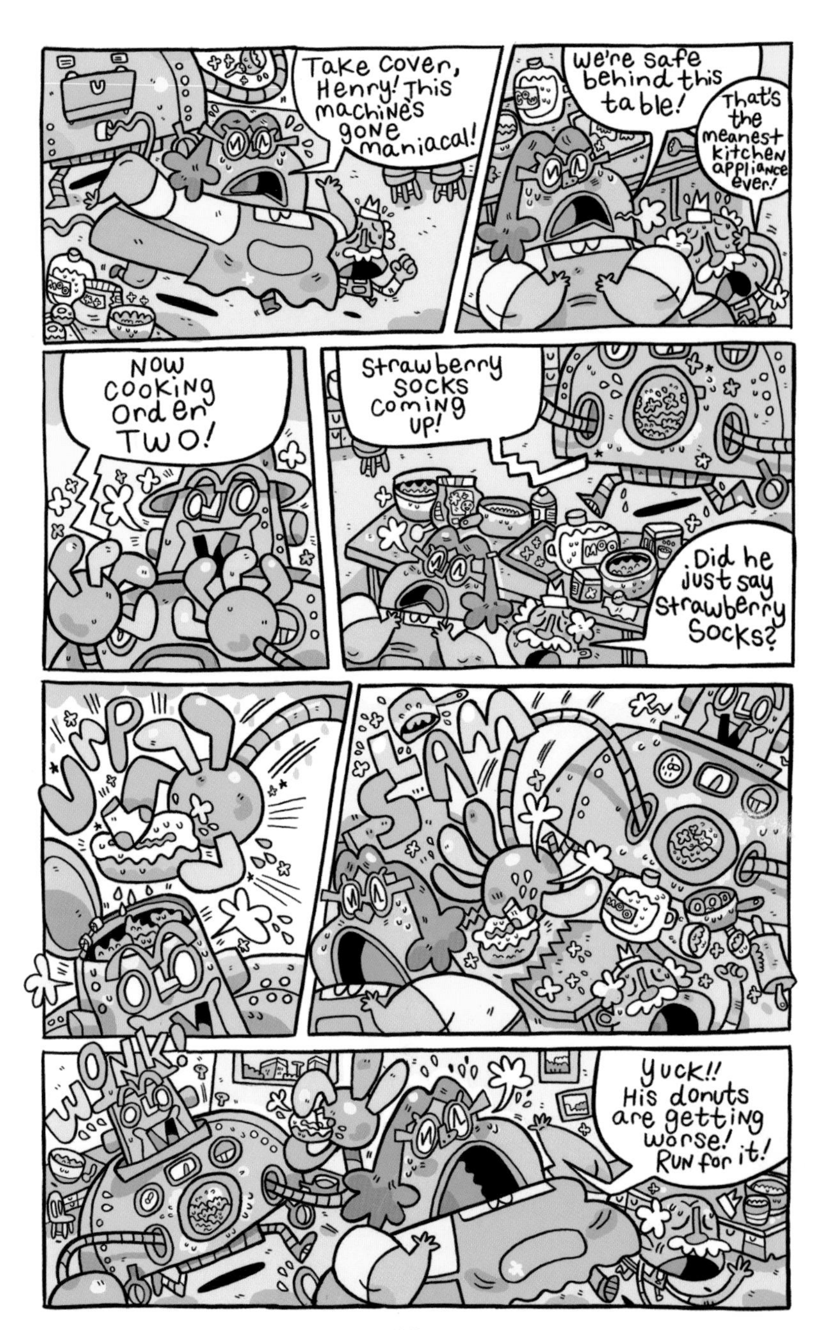
Take cover, Henry! This machine's gone maniacal!
We're safe behind this table!
That's the meanest kitchen appliance ever!
NOW COOKING Order TWO!
Strawberry socks coming up!
Did he just say Strawberry Socks?
VRRP
SLAM
WONK!
Yuck!! His donuts are getting worse! RUN for it!

Who's ready for order Three?
Please enjoy: rotten fruit toppings! Get 'em while they're hot!
Eek! It's raining nasty donuts!
I've had enough! Let's show Mr. Baker we can fight back too!
Have a drink, Mr. Baker!
DONK!
Nice shot, Big mama!
Operation error!
BZZZZZT!

Hey, MR. Baker! No use crying over spilt milk! HAHAHA!
zzt
zzt
Oh! Good one! I'll remember that LINE for next time!
HA HA! you also could've said, "MR. Baker, that was quite a splash!"

Sensors destroyed! I'm not supposed to get wet!
ZZZZ!
Oh NO! That robot is going bonkers!
He is SPINNING out of control! What do we do now?
STOMP!
STOMP!
MR. Baker is RUNNING right towards the wall at full Speed!!!

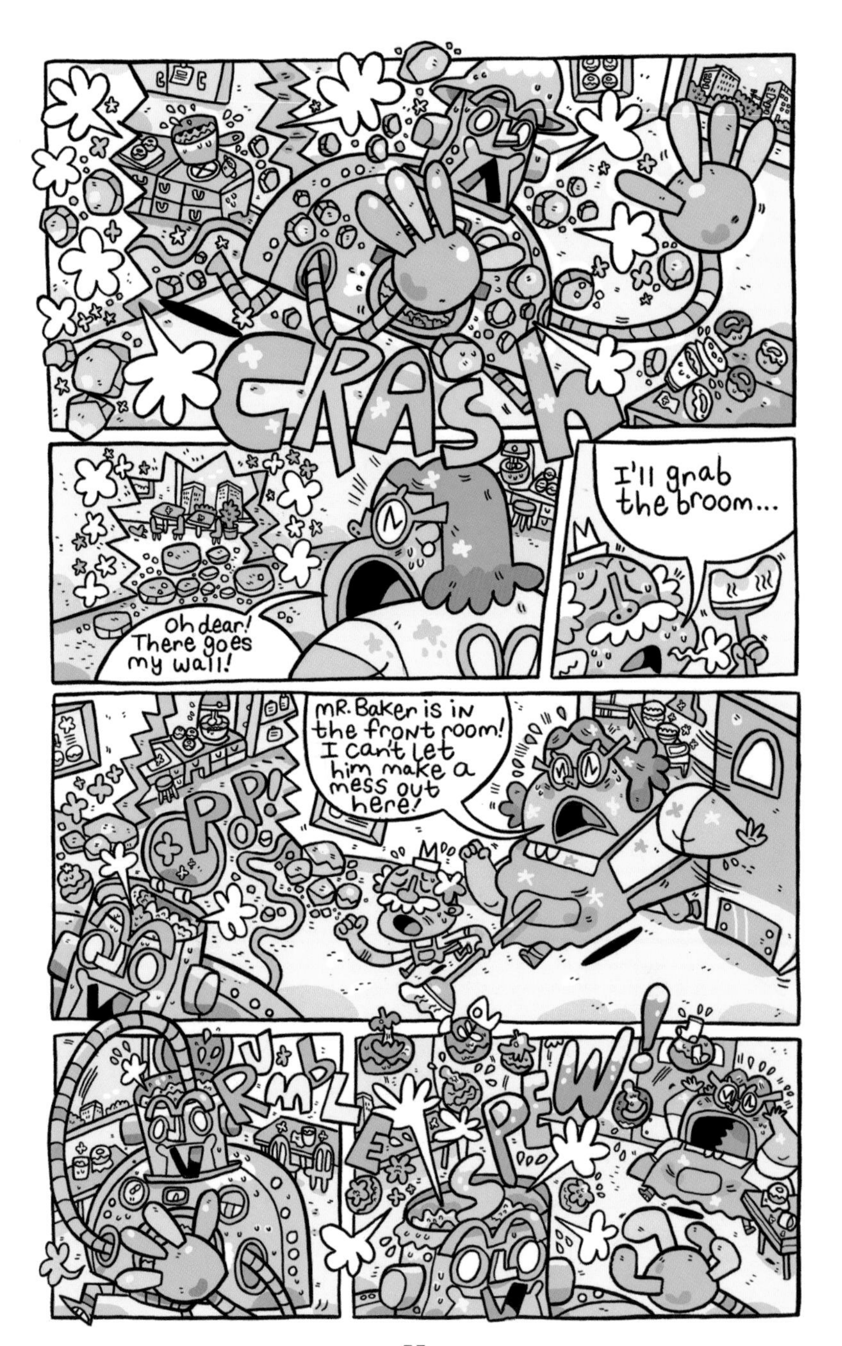
CRASH
Oh dear! There goes my wall!
I'll grab the broom...
POP!
MR. Baker is in the front room! I can't let him make a mess out here!
RUMBLE
SPEW!

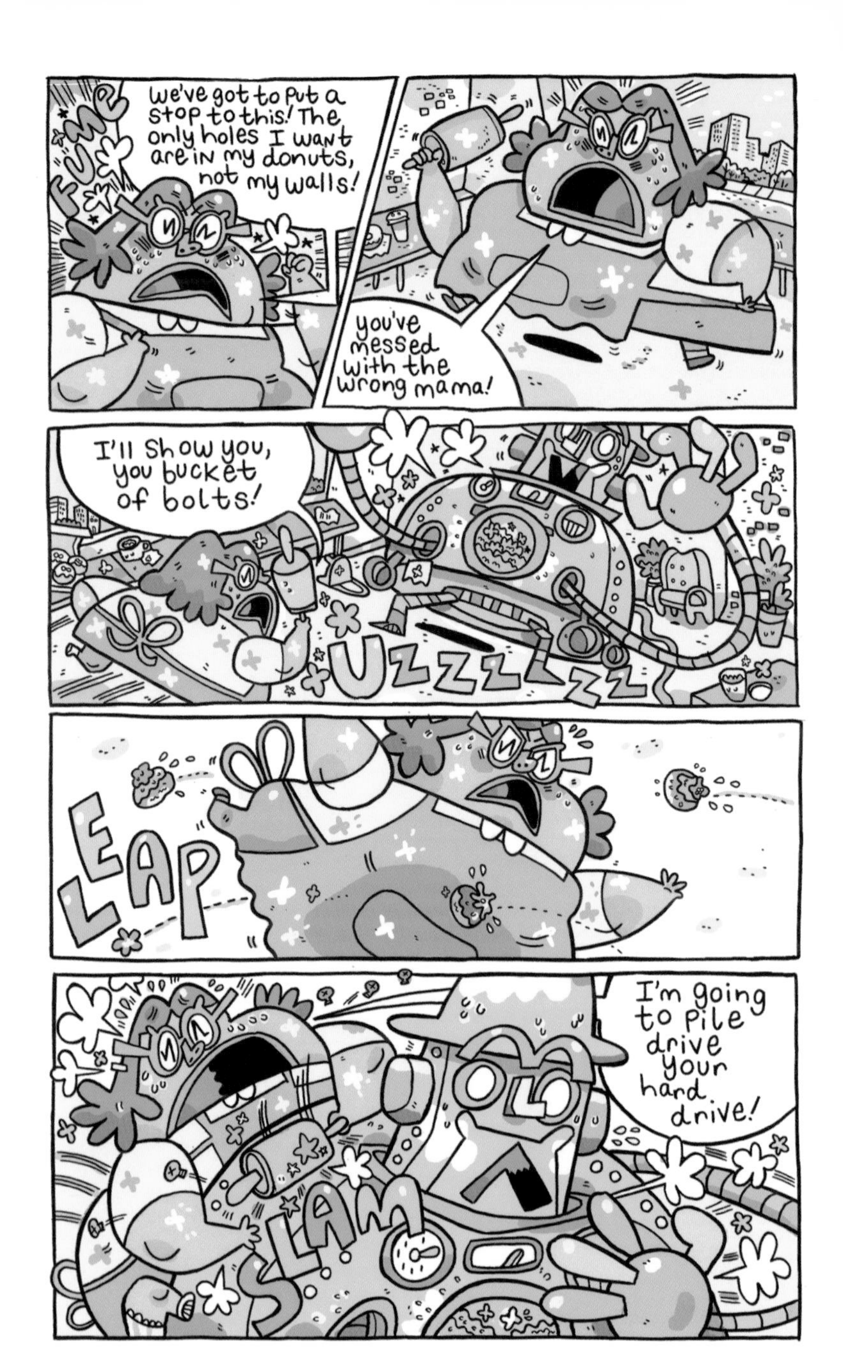
FUME
We've got to put a stop to this! The only holes I want are in my donuts, not my walls!
You've messed with the wrong mama!
I'll show you, you bucket of bolts!
UZZZZZZ
LEAP
I'm going to pile drive your hard drive!
SLAM

whoooaaa! you put me down this very instant!!
WONK
WONK
SPLAT!
oof!
Well, that didn't work!

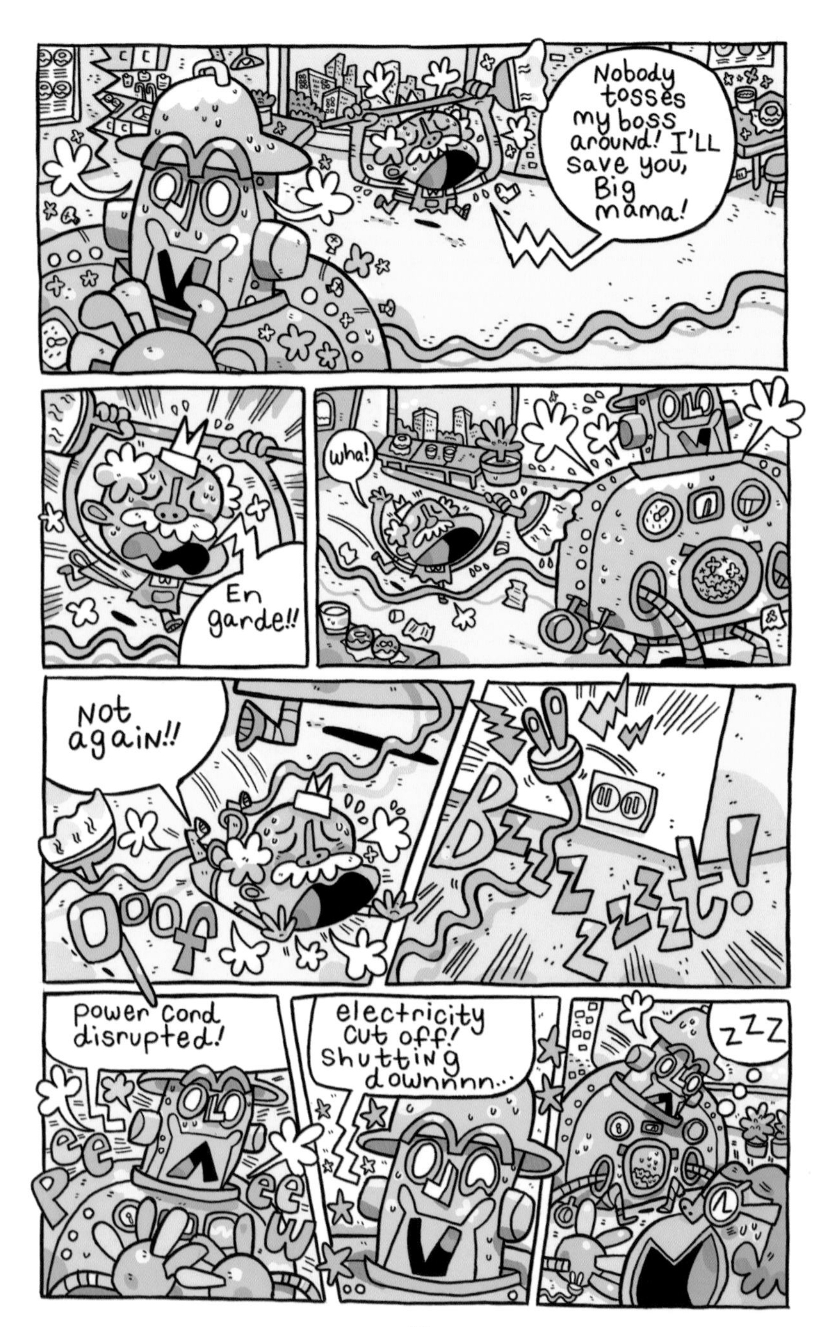

Nobody tosses my boss around! I'LL save you, Big mama!
En garde!!
wha!
Not again!!
Ooof
Bzzzzzzzt!
power cord disrupted!
Peeeew
electricity cut off! shutting downnnn...
zZZ

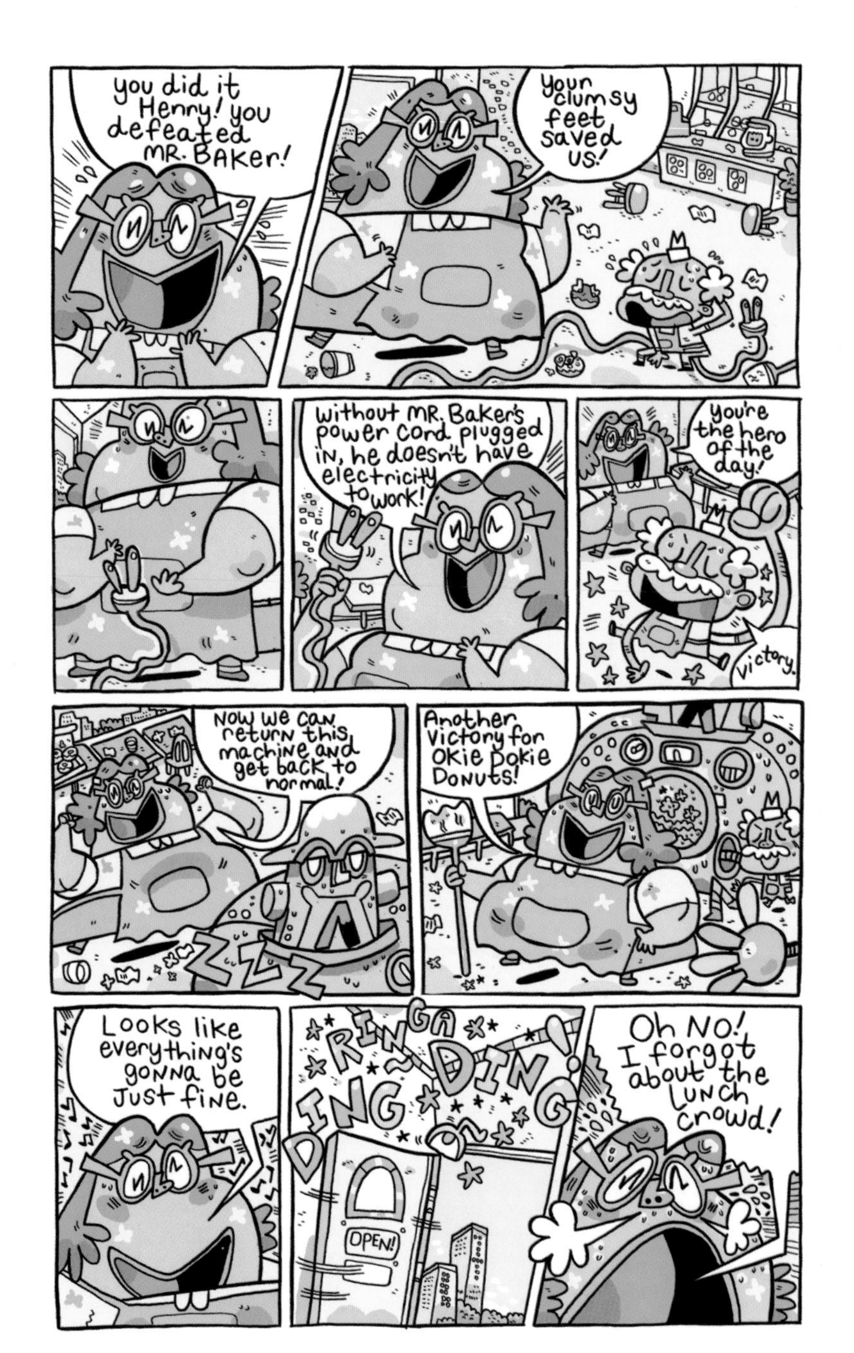
you did it Henry! you defeated MR. BAKER!
Your clumsy feet saved US!
without MR. Baker's power cord plugged in, he doesn't have electricity to work!
you're the hero of the day!
victory.
NOW WE CAN return this machine and get back to normal!
Another Victory for Okie Dokie Donuts!
Looks like everything's gonna be just fine.
RING A DING DING DING!
OPEN!
Oh NO! I forgot about the lunch crowd!

my good-ness!
OhHELLO!
Hello, Big mama! I'm back!
I see the machine is working out! You even moved him to the front room, Neat!
Wanted to show him off, eh?
I don't blame you. He is rather impressive isn't he?
SIZZLE
Are you kidding me? That machine went nuts and threw smelly donuts at my face!
MR. Baker is easily excitable! over time, you'll learn to love him!

Besides, I haven't even told you about the latest deal...
If you act now, I can throw in these great attachments!
The icing hat!
The handy extra arms!
and Zoom Zoom roller Skates!
with all this and more, MR. Baker will be the duke of danish!
King of cakes! Prince of Pastries!! Everyone will want to eat his donuts!
No DeaL! That machine is too much! I like doing things the old way! and so do my customers!
YEAH!

Oh please, Big mama!
MR. Baker can make a donut way more delicious than yours!
GASP!
I'll Prove it, too! I'll eat a MR. Baker donut right here, right now!
GROWL
NO way!! I won't allow it!!!
His donuts aren't for eating!
I said I want a donut...
STOMP
...and I want it right NOW!!!
Very WELL MR. Mayweather.

WINK
Heh Heh Heh...
you want a donut?
Serve yourself!

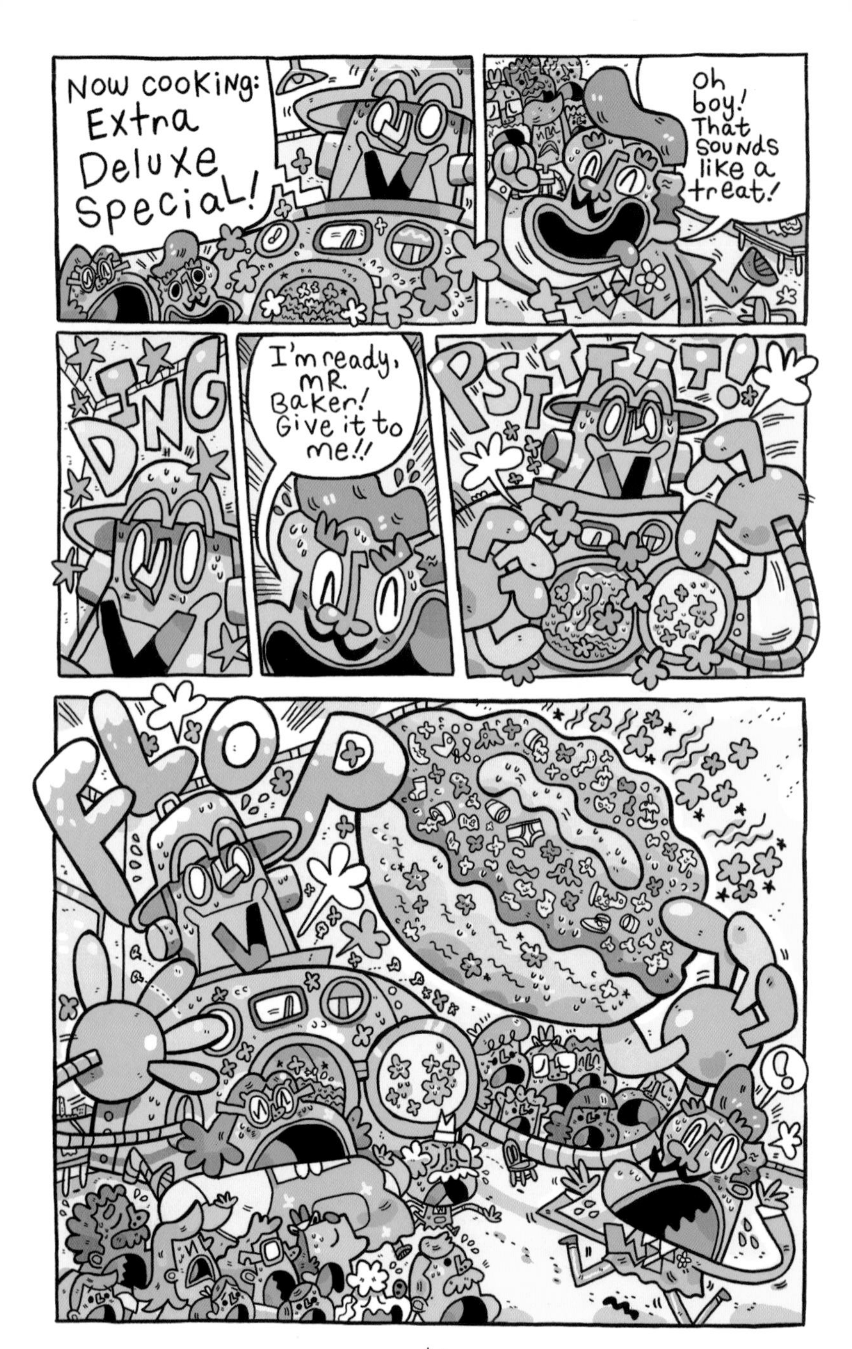
Now cooking: Extra Deluxe Special!
Oh boy! That sounds like a treat!
DING
I'm ready, Mr. Baker! Give it to me!!
PSTTTTT!
FLOP
!

Yikes! It's a giant garbage donut!
Get that thing away from me!!!
PLOP!
GULP
I can't believe he ate that big mess in one bite!
YUCK!
That was just awful!

Ooohhh! you win, Big mama!
Looks like you do make the best donuts in town!
That giant wreck was just wrong!
MR. Baker is strong, fast, and an amazing deal...
... but now I see that donuts must be crafted with a gentle hand!
Now he gets it!!!
BOP
I'm glad to hear that, MR. mayweather!

That clunky machine's digitized delicacies could never replicate the care I put into each donut!
Good food takes time and consideration!
I'll make my donuts by hand, now and forever! And that's the way we lik'em!
Right ON! Big ma! Big ma!
Oh, I guess there's nothing for me here...
except... Big mama?
yes?
Can I get a box of your donuts?
Please! Oh Please!

Sure! But you have to get to the back of the line!
HA HA
HA HA HA!
STOMP STOMP
Aw! Butter Sticks!!
Alrighty! Who's first?
Step right up! Free frosting for every-one!
Yum!
I told ya, this place was good!
OKIE DOKIE DONUTS
The End

My name is Chris Eliopoulos. I am a illustrator and cartoonist from Chicago, IL. Thank you for reading my comic book. I hope you enjoyed it. Drawing comics is a lot of fun!

Special thank you to Michael Deforge, Annie, mom, Dad, Kim, Sheldon Vella, Brett Warnock, Chris Staros, Leigh Walton, Robert Venditti, and Bob Boyle, for all the help and support while making this book!

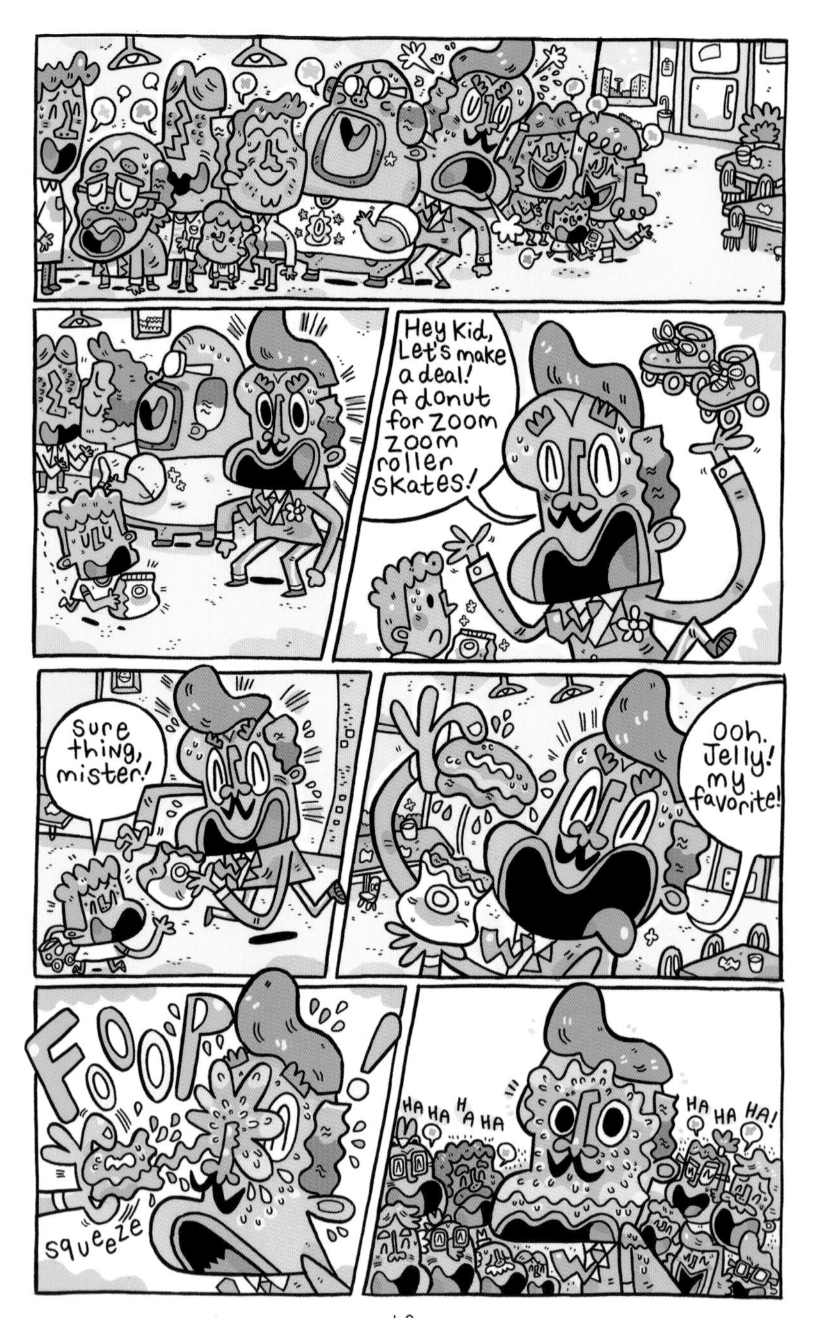
Hey Kid, Let's make a deal! A donut for ZOOM ZOOM roller skates!
Sure thing, mister!
Ooh. Jelly! my favorite!
FOOOP!
squeeze
HA HA HA HA
HA HA HA!